Translated by Susan Beard

First published in Swedish in 2012
as *Jul I Stora Skogen* by Rabén & Sjögren
First published in English in 2014 by Floris Books
© 2012 Rabén & Sjögren
English version © 2014 Floris Books
All rights reserved. No part of this publication may be reproduced without
the prior permission of Floris Books, 15 Harrison Gardens, Edinburgh
www.florisbooks.co.uk

British Library CIP Data available
ISBN 978-178250-136-7
Printed in Europe

The Yule Tomte and the Little Rabbits

*In Swedish tradition it is a tomte (or jultomte – Yule tomte)
who brings Christmas presents to children. It is traditional to
leave a bowl of porridge out for the tomte on Christmas
night as a special gift to thank him.*

*The 13th of December is St Lucia's Day, and in Sweden,
saffron buns are made to celebrate this holiday.*

The Yule Tomte and the Little Rabbits

A Christmas Story for Advent

Ulf Stark and Eva Eriksson

Floris Books

1

Grump the tomte lived in the grounds of an empty cottage and every day, he slipped into the cottage through the cat flap.

That's how small he was. Real house tomtes are like that. They are small and quick and grumpy and they are always dressed in grey, apart from a pointy red hat. You hardly ever see them.

Every day Grump took a walk through the cottage, even though no one lived there any more. No one had lived there for fifty years. He made sure everything was as it should be. He had a little rest on the bed, he pulled the roller blinds up and down, and best of all, he had a quick ride on the rocking horse.

The last thing he did was wind up the big wall clock. It was difficult because he couldn't reach it, but house tomtes are very particular about time, so Grump had built himself a ladder. He had just climbed to the very top rung when he heard a buzzing sound.

"Bzzz, bzzz!" it went. "I'm stuck. Save me!"

It was a bumble-bee, trapped in the spider's web in the window. The more it moved, the more tangled it became.

"Well, you had no business being there in the first place!" said Grump. "You will just have to wait until I have finished with the clock!"

He grunted. Because house tomtes, as you know, are very grouchy.

But soon he climbed down the ladder and untangled the bee from the web.

"Great. Now I have to look after you as well," he complained to the bee. "I can't leave you to lie here and freeze until Christmas."

Then he looked at the clock.

"And you have made me late!"

"Late for what?" asked the bee.

"For lighting the candle, of course. It's all your fault!"

Grump picked up the bee and ran back to his own house to light the first candle in the Advent candlestick. Tomtes always light the first candle on the first of December, whatever day of the week it falls on.

"How pretty! And how lovely and warm it is," yawned the bee, sitting on Grump's lap and staring into the flame. "What shall we do tomorrow?"

"Nothing," said Grump. "You are going to go to sleep and keep quiet."

"All right, then," said the bee, and fell asleep.

2

Grump got up early the next morning. He always got up early.

He washed his mittens and went outside to hang them up to dry. It was still dark, although the moon was shining brightly. Grump put on his boots and lit the candle in his lantern.

He stopped beside the box where he had made a bed for the bee the day before, with moss for a mattress and a leaf for a sheet. He pulled off the leaf and prodded the bee. He kept prodding it until it woke up.

"You're awake! Didn't I tell you to go to sleep?" he said to the bee crossly. "Oh well, I suppose you will have to come out with me now."

"Bzzz," yawned the bee.

Grump put the bee into his lantern. It was like a little glass house for the bee, and the warmth from the candle was just right.

Grump hung his mittens on the clothes line. Then he nodded towards the stable.

"A horse called Stella used to live there," Grump said. "Once she knocked me over with a swish of her tail. And I had to chase off all the horse flies. What hard work that was!"

Then he walked past the empty pigsty.

"And this is where Porky lived. He was always grunting and wanting his neck tickled. Good job he's gone."

Finally, he showed the bee the chicken house.

"Not to mention those good-for-nothing chickens! What a racket they made! And every day they ran off and hid their eggs, just to be awkward!"

He stood still, looking at the empty buildings and wiping his nose.

"Well, let's go in," he said. 'I just wanted to make sure no one had tried to come back."

They walked back to the dog kennel where Grump lived. It was just the right size for a house tomte. He had made it very nice inside, with a table and chairs, a door and windows, and a wood stove from a dolls' house.

Grump picked up the bee, blew out the lantern and lit the Advent candle instead.

"Can I go back to sleep now?" buzzed the bee.

"No. We are going to do some reading," snapped Grump. "And you are going to be quiet and listen, so that you can learn something."

He got out his best book. It was the only one he had. It was called *In Praise of Solitude.* Then he started to read:

"What could be better than enjoying silence all alone…"

He did not get any further because he heard a soft humming sound. It was the bee, who had fallen asleep and was snoring and dreaming about summer.

"Well, that just about does it," muttered Grump. "Can't a person get a bit of peace and quiet in his own home?"

The next day was not quiet, either.

Because that was when the wind came. It sounded like a huge organ playing. It whistled through all the cracks in the kennel. It shook the trees, sending pine cones and acorns pattering onto the kennel's roof.

"I can't get a minute's peace!" complained Grump to the sleeping bee.

But the bee didn't wake up, even when Grump shook it. Then Grump remembered his grey mittens hanging on the washing line.

"What if they blow away?" he thought.

He reached the washing line just as the wind flew off with the mittens, whisking them high above the pigsty and the woodshed.

They waved at Grump as if they were teasing him.

"Come back!" he called.

They didn't come back. Grump turned his face to the wind and waved his fist in the air.

"This is no way to behave!" he shouted. "You should be ashamed of yourself!"

Then the wind grabbed his red tomte hat and blew it away in the same direction as the mittens.

Grump ran after his hat, all the way to the gate, but he wasn't quick enough.

"I don't care about my hat!" he shouted in a rage. "I'm not going to be a tomte any more!"

And he gave the gate a kick.

The people who lived in the house many years ago had attached a sign to the gate. The sign came loose and flew off too.

The sign had said TOMTE COTTAGE – until a squirrel chewed away a corner of it. Now all it said was TOMTE CO.

"Might as well go inside," thought Grump to himself. "I'll go in and shut the door, and I won't open it for anyone. And if the bee says anything, I won't answer. I won't celebrate Christmas. I won't do anything. I won't look after anyone. I will sit here in my little hut and enjoy the peace and quiet all on my own."

He left a sugar cube next to the bee for when it woke up.

4

Quite some way away, under an enormous oak tree in a big forest, was a rabbit burrow. The burrow was full of life.

Mother Rabbit was cooking cabbage juice. Auntie Bunty was polishing winter apples, wrapping them in sycamore leaves, and putting them away in a corner. Uncle Nubbin was doing his exercises. Father Rabbit was brushing his black hat. And Grandfather Rabbit was thinking. He liked thinking. At that moment he was thinking about why things went downwards when they fell.

And the children? Well, they were rushing around, being noisy.

They were playing shipwreck, taking long hops from one piece of root furniture to the next without touching the ground.

Then Mother, who wanted some peace, said:

"Can't you go outside and play, while you still can? It will be winter soon."

"What is winter?" asked Binny.

None of the rabbit children knew what winter was. They had never experienced a winter.

"It's when the cold gets so cold it pinches your nose and everything turns as white as a cauliflower," said Grandfather. "The white stuff is called snow."

"Then I will go outside and wait for the snow," said Binny.

"You do that," said Uncle Nubbin.

"I'll come with you," said Barty.

"Mind you don't get blown away," Mother said. "There's an awfully strong wind today."

The rest of the rabbit children stayed inside and practised their indoor hopping, but Binny and Barty went outside.

5

Outside, it was blowing so hard it made Binny and Barty's ears flap. They chased leaves that were whirling about in the wind.

"First to catch that big leaf is the winner!" shouted Binny.

She pointed to the biggest leaf of all. They both hopped as high as they could to catch it, but every time they hopped, the wind caught hold of it again. They ran further and further away from their burrow.

After a while Barty called out.

"Look over here!"

He had found the tomte's hat in among the moss.

"It looks like a kind of hat," Binny said.

Barty tried to put it on his head, but his ears got in the way.

"Let's take it with us," said Binny. "It could be good to put things in."

"What kind of things?" said Barty.

"These kind of things," said Binny.

She pointed at the tomte's two mittens that had blown away. They were caught in a juniper bush. They sat there, waving at her. She reached up to get them, and put them on her ears.

"Look! Ear warmers," she laughed. "Lovely warm ear warmers. Come on, let's run home and show Grandfather."

"Yes, these will give him something new to think about!" Barty said.

On the way home they found another thing: a four-sided thing with squiggles on it. Well, it wasn't really four-sided, because someone had chewed off one corner.

"What's this?" Binny wondered.

"Perhaps it's winter?" guessed Barty. "It is quite white."

"Yes," said Binny, "but it is mostly grey. And it is not pinching our noses."

"No, I suppose not, but let's take it anyway."

And they ran off home with their discoveries.

6

Grandfather turned the tomte hat this way and that. He lifted it up and then dropped it. It fell in a little red heap on the ground.

"It does at least fall downwards," he said.

"Yes, but what is it?" asked Binny.

Grandfather waved the hat about wildly. Then everyone had a go at blowing on it. It flapped a little.

"It is a flag," he said at last, sounding very sure of himself. "A red flag that should go on the end of a stick."

"And what about these?" asked Barty, holding up the mittens.

"Perhaps we could use them to keep peas in," said Mother.

"Yes, or to dust a hat with," suggested Father.

"No, they are sleeping bags," Grandfather said.

"Sleeping bags? What are they?" asked Uncle Nubbin.

"You put little children in them at night time," explained Grandfather.

"Like… mouse children, you mean?" asked Binny.

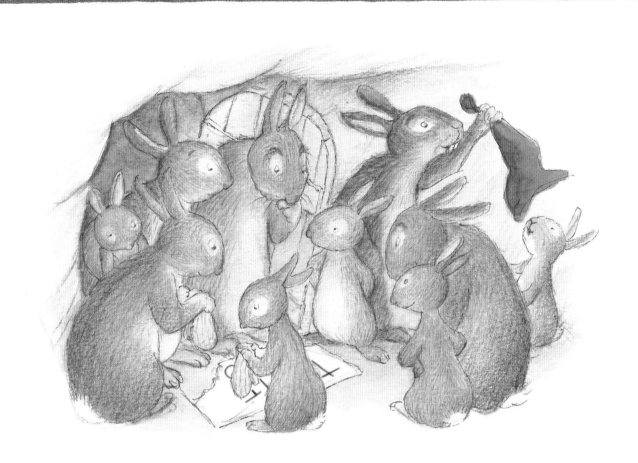

"Yes. Precisely. Mouse children," said Grandfather, pleased with himself.

"It seems like you know practically everything," said Auntie Bunty.

But Grandfather did not understand the sign.

"Perhaps it is a door," he said thoughtfully. "With a name on. But it is best if we ask Owl. He can read."

They decided to go and see Owl the following day.

7

Owl lived in a tree with a hole in it. He slept there during the day because he liked to read all night. At least, he liked to read all night when the moon was shining. Or so he said.

The rabbits carried the sign to him. On the way, a squirrel and some forest mice joined them. And two jackdaws.

"Hello! Hello, Owl!" called Binny.

At first she called quietly, and then she and Barty called much louder.

Then they all shouted together as loudly as they could: "OWL!"

Owl looked out. He gave himself a shake and blinked, first one eye and then the other.

"What is this all about?" he hooted crossly.

"Why didn't you answer?" asked the rabbits.

"I was sleeping," he said. "And I do not speak in my sleep."

"You're not hungry, are you?" asked the mice anxiously.

"No, but I am sleepy. Oh my moon and stars, why have you woken me up in the middle of the day?"

"We were wondering what this is. And whether it says anything that can be read. If you can read, that is," said Grandfather.

They put the sign on the ground with the squiggles facing upwards. Owl sat on a branch and looked at it for a long time.

"Perhaps it is something very important," said Mother. "Something that…"

"No, it is not," Owl said quickly. "It is just a normal kind of thing. A thing with a few letters on it. F and P and all sorts of other things. Good day!"

And he flapped up in the air and disappeared into his hole.

A moment later he stuck his head out.

"And do not wake me up again," he cried, slamming his door shut.

"Well, that's that," sighed Grandfather. "A perfectly normal kind of thing."

"I was hoping it would be something exciting," said Mother. "Something that meant an adventure."

"Yes, that would have been nice," agreed Uncle Nubbin.

"Don't pay any attention to Owl," croaked one of the jackdaws.

"No, he can't read. Not a single letter," said the other jackdaw.

"What does it say, then?" asked Binny.

"Yes, what does it say?" asked the squirrel and the mice and all the others.

The jackdaws swaggered up and down over the letters with their heads bent. Sometimes there was the sound of a T, sometimes an O.

"What does it say *all together*?" Barty asked impatiently.

"TOMTE," laughed one jackdaw.

"CO," said the other.

There was a moment of silence. Then Binny spoke.

"What is a tomte?" she asked.

"A tomte comes at Christmas. The Yule Tomte," said the first jackdaw.

"And what is Christmas?" Mother asked.

"We have no idea, but it sounds exciting," the second jackdaw replied.

"A proper adventure," agreed number one.

Then they flew up into the air, laughing.

Jackdaws think almost everything is funny.

The next day, the squirrel came to visit the rabbits.

"Now I know!" he panted excitedly, before he had even got through the door.

"People usually knock," said Grandfather. "And say hello. Sit down and take a deep breath. Then you can tell us what you know."

The squirrel said hello and sat down in one of the wicker chairs.

Uncle Nubbin served him a glass of pine needle juice.

"Well, what do you know?" asked Grandfather.

"I know what Christmas is," said the squirrel proudly.

"And where did you find that out?" asked Grandfather.

He was cross because the squirrel, who was so young, knew something that he didn't know.

"I found out about it from Grandma's uncle. He is ancient."

"And what did he have to say?"

"He said that at Christmas you hang pretty things on a tree. And you eat and dance. And sing. And give presents."

"Are you absolutely sure about that?" asked Grandfather.

"Yes. He heard it from some people who were in the forest sawing down a perfectly good climbing and jumping tree."

"And did your relative by any chance say when this Christmas takes place?"

"'When the tomte comes', he said."

"We had better get started straight away," said Grandfather.

"But surely you don't think the Yule Tomte is coming here?" said Mother.

"Didn't it say TOMTE CO?'" said Grandfather. "I have thought, and CO must mean COMING!"

10

Soon all the animals in the Big Forest knew that the Yule Tomte was coming.

The voles knew it, and the badger. Even the worms down in the ground were talking about it, although they were supposed to be sleeping. And the birds in the treetops.

"He is coming soon, coming soon," they twittered.

But they knew very little about this Yule Tomte.

"He probably works very hard and has to come a long way," said Uncle Nubbin.

"Oh yes," said Mother Rabbit eagerly. "Poor tomte. We should give him lots of presents when he comes."

"And perhaps sing him a song," exclaimed Grandfather.

"What song?" asked Binny.

"A tomte song, of course. A joyful song to make him happy and forget all his worries."

"And who will make it up?"

"I will," said Grandfather. "I will go and think about it straight away."

"Yes, and he must have all sorts of treats," said Auntie Bunty.

"And food!" cackled both the jackdaws.

"And presentations," cooed a pigeon.

"Presentations?" said Father.

"Yes. That is what I've heard, anyway," said the pigeon, who took a trip to town now and again. "That is what you do at Christmas. Everyone says so."

"That doesn't sound quite right," said Uncle Nubbin.

"Well," said the pigeon, "it is only what I've heard."

Then it flew away, flapping its wings, hoping it hadn't said something silly.

But the voles practised presenting themselves to each other over and over, giggling:

"May I present myself to you, Mr Tomte?"

Grandfather sat in a corner, working on his song.

He wrote the word 'snow'.

But then he rubbed it out again.

All over the forest, everyone was getting ready because the Yule Tomte was coming.

Uncle Nubbin washed his ears. Rabbits are very particular about that.

Auntie Bunty made a party hat from a piece of moss and a twig of rowan berries.

The rabbit children practised presenting themselves.

Mother Rabbit dusted the furniture with a cloth.

And Father Rabbit sat with his black hat on his head, wondering how you actually greet a tomte.

Father Rabbit called to Mother Rabbit.

"Listen to this: 'Here he is at last, our dear tomte.' Can I say that? Or is it better to say: 'Oh, how pleased we are to see you, Mr Tomte!'"

"I am sure either would do fine," said Mother. "But can't we just say: 'Good day'?"

"No, no," answered Father. "That is far too simple. It has to be something very special. And what if he comes in the evening? Then it would not do at all to say 'Good day'."

He stood in front of the mirror, took off his hat, bowed, and said politely:

"You are most heartily welcome, dear tomte."

Then he turned to his wife and asked: "How did that sound?"

"Very special. Now we do not have to worry about it any longer."

"Good," said Father. "Then I will go outside and put the flag beside the entrance. It will look most welcoming."

And that is what he did.

Mother carried on dusting the furniture, as she muttered: "Oh, how exciting this is, how exciting this is."

12

Mother Rabbit was worried, in an excited kind of way. What would the Yule Tomte – whatever he looked like – enjoy eating?

She sat in the kitchen with Mrs Hare and the squirrel, and Mrs Hedgehog, who had woken from her winter sleep, drinking tea and wondering what to offer.

"Snails are always tasty," yawned the hedgehog.

"Something with nuts," suggested the squirrel. "Perhaps a dish of pine nut cakes with blueberry jam."

"It will have to be a little bit of everything," said Mother. "A help-yourself."

"Yes, or a hop-yourself," said Binny, hopping about.

She hopped so much that Mrs Hare's teacup bounced on to the floor.

"Stop! We need all our cups and plates for the party," scolded Mother. "Go outside if you are going to carry on like that. I can't think with all your jumping."

Binny hung her head and left.

She felt sorry about the teacup, but she felt even more sorry for herself. She was sad and angry, because Mother sounded so cross.

But as she stepped outside the burrow something fell on to her nose. Something cold that made her sneeze and laugh. The air around her was full of white flakes. They fluttered down and settled on the ground, on the branches and on her.

She picked up as much snow as she could hold in her hands and threw it over her head.

She leapt about with joy.

"Snow!" she shouted. "It must be snow!"

She danced a now-it's-snowing dance until she slipped over.

Then she poked her head into the burrow and called out:

"There is snow out here and my paws are all slippy! Come out and slide about, everybody!"

13

Back in the dog kennel at Tomte Cottage, Grump lay in his bed looking out of the window and listening to the bee's buzzy snore.

All day yesterday it had snowed, but now the sky was full of stars. One of them was shining more brightly than the others.

"Annoying star!" thought Grump. "It's shining so brightly I can't sleep!"

Then he fell asleep.

Unseen, the star seemed to glide down from the sky. Slowly but surely it dropped towards the farm and the dog kennel.

It hovered over the very top of the flagpole, then sank past the white branches of the apple tree and down towards the window.

But by this time it was no longer a star.

It was a woman in a white dress, with wings on her back and a crown of candles on her head. The candles shone with a dazzling light.

The woman walked into the kennel, holding a tray.

"Do not be afraid," she said.

"I'm not afraid, I'm angry!" said Grump. "Can't you see I am trying to sleep?"

"I have coffee and saffron buns and ginger biscuits," the woman continued. "And I have some good news to tell you."

"And what might that be?" asked Grump suspiciously.

"You are going to have a family."

"What on earth are you talking about? Am I going to have a child?"

"No, two."

"I don't want any children. I want to be alone! Do you hear?"

"I hear," said the woman. "You can say whatever you like, but you are going to have them anyway. Take a ginger biscuit and be good. Happy Christmas!"

"I don't want to be good. And I don't want Christmas! Not ever!" bellowed Grump.

But the woman had already gone.

14

What a stupid dream, thought Grump when he woke up the next morning and remembered the woman with the wings.

But on the stool beside his bed was a coffee cup and a plate with buns and a ginger biscuit.

He drank the coffee, even though it was cold, and ate the buns and the ginger biscuit. Then he hid the plate under the bed.

"So much for that dream," he said. "All gone now."

Then he went outside.

Snow was glittering on the roof. It was so cold that Grump could see his own breath. His ears were freezing.

"And I haven't even got a hat," he grumbled. "I must find something to put on my head, otherwise my ears will drop off with the cold."

He slipped into the cottage through the cat flap. In a cupboard he found a sock that had been left behind. It was grey with red trim. He put it on.

Back in his own house, he woke the bee up by shaking it for a long time. He gave it a few biscuit crumbs and some pieces of crunchy sugar left over from the buns.

"Mmm," hummed the bee. "This tastes heavenly!"

"Don't talk rubbish," said Grump. "I don't want to hear a word about heaven. Or children! Or Christmas, either. Have you seen how ridiculous I look with a sock on my head?"

"Yes," buzzed the bee.

"And before you ask, I don't believe in angels! Would you like some tea? We might as well have a cup, seeing as how you have woken up and are bothering me."

But by the time the water had boiled, the bee had gone back to sleep.

15

In the forest everybody was working very hard to get everything ready for the Yule Tomte.

"Just as long as he doesn't turn up before the toffee is ready," said Auntie Bunty, pouring pine resin into small cases.

"No, that would be a fine how-do-you-do," panted Mother Rabbit. She was in a terrible rush, cooking and cleaning.

Uncle Nubbin asked the voles and the badger for help to make the burrow bigger. They started digging a big hall so there would be room for everyone at the party. Earth and roots flew about everywhere.

They whistled, too, and disturbed Grandfather while he was trying to make up a Christmas song. So far he only had two lines:

Oh, snow so white and night so clear,
Such fun, Mr Tomte, to have you here.

He was especially pleased with the 'Oh' at the beginning.

"Can't you be a little quieter?" he pleaded. "I am trying to think of a rhyme!"

Father Rabbit was looking at his hat. He had brushed it with a special brush to make it shine. He thought he might give it to the Yule Tomte. That would be a splendid present.

Perhaps a little too splendid. After all, the hat was his favourite thing.

"I think I'll give him the flag instead," he told Binny. "Don't you think he will find that much more fun? It's red and flaps about in the wind."

"Yes, perhaps," said Binny.

"Then I will go and get it immediately."

He put his hat on top of the cupboard where he always kept it, and went out. Binny sat with her chin in her paws, thinking. "But what about me? What shall I give to the Yule Tomte?"

16

The grown-ups were busy with their preparations. They wanted the children to be outside, amusing themselves.

So all the children gathered together and slid down the slope. They slid on their tummies, on their backs and on their bottoms. And sometimes they held on tight to each other's feet and made a long, wriggly snake.

Today the snow was soft enough to make snowballs, so they had a snowball fight. Uncle Nubbin showed them how to pack the snow tight into a ball.

"I learnt this when I was a little rabbit," he said.

First they saw who could throw the farthest. Binny's big sister, Abby, won.

Then they threw snowballs at each other.

Everyone except Binny. She was still wondering what she could give the tomte to make him really happy. She sighed. She couldn't think of a thing.

Right at that moment a snowball landed on her neck.

"Oops," said Barty.

"Thank you," said Binny.

"Why are you saying thank you?"

"Because I've just had a good idea."

"What?" asked Barty.

"I'm not telling," said Binny. "It's a secret."

Binny sat down on a stump behind a fir tree, where she couldn't be seen. She picked up a lump of snow. Carefully, she shaped it with her paws to give it a sweet little nose, a round tummy, arms, legs and ears. Then she added a small ball for a tail. The ears were the hardest. They kept falling off.

At last she was finished.

She was delighted. Her snow rabbit was so lovely. It was quite possibly the best thing she had ever made. She sat for a long time, holding it in her arms.

"Oh, how happy the Yule Tomte will be," she thought to herself.

17

When it started to get dark, Binny took her snow rabbit into the burrow, so that none of the night animals would trample on it. Without anyone seeing, she climbed up on a stool and put it inside Father's hat.

Tomorrow she would put it in a box and wrap it round with lingonberry stalks.

But after she went to bed, Binny began to think that it might be a long time before the tomte came. She really wanted to show someone her snow rabbit *now*.

She wanted Grandfather to turn it this way and that, and mutter: "Well, bless my eyes, what a surprise!"

She wanted the other children to be envious, and she wanted Father to stroke her ears and tell her she was the cleverest bunny of all.

"I'll show it to them first thing tomorrow," she thought.

When she woke up next morning everyone else was already up. *My snow rabbit!* she thought, and she leapt out of bed, calling:

"Wait until you see! You won't believe it!"

"What is it, dear?" asked Mother.

"Get out your hat, Father!"

"Why, if I may ask?" said Father.

"Just do it!" said Binny.

So Father went to the cupboard. He was certainly very surprised when he looked inside his hat.

"Water," he said, in an unusually deep voice.

"What did you say?" asked Auntie Bunty.

"She has poured water in my hat," sighed Father.

Then he turned to Binny.

"How could you? You know how much I cared about that hat!"

"It was a rabbit made of snow," she sobbed. "It was for the tomte."

"And now it has melted, and the water has damaged the hat," said Father, in a voice almost as sad as Binny's. He stood still, holding the hat. It made a sploshing sound.

Binny went outside. She wanted to be alone.

18

After a lot of work, the Christmas tree was ready.

The waxwings pecked off twigs of frozen rowan berries and hung them here and there. The jackdaws came with wild red apples. The magpie brought along all kinds of things it found on its travels: bits of glass, bottle tops, and pieces of silver foil. The tree was also full of colourful feathers that the birds had plucked from their own plumage.

Oh, how beautiful it was! And what fun it would be to dance around it and sing songs. But they couldn't do that until the Yule Tomte arrived.

"He is in no particular hurry, that one," said Uncle Nubbin.

"No, and the food is all ready and waiting," said Auntie Bunty.

"Can't we eat it anyway?" asked the voles.

"Yes! We will think of the tomte while we are eating!" said the badger.

But Auntie Bunty would not hear of it. Neither would Mother.

"We will have to wait," she said firmly, and she took a bite of one of the sour wild apples. It did not make her any happier.

"That slowcoach tomte!" she burst out, stamping her foot. "And to think we have made presents."

"And I brushed my hat as best I could, considering the water damage," said Father.

"And my song is nearly ready," said Grandfather.

But the children weren't cross. They made up a new game. They ran into the burrow shouting:

"The tomte is here, he's here!"

Then they laughed so much that they got hiccups when Father ran to get his hat and Grandfather started singing:

"Oh, snow so white and night so clear…"

19

The fifth time the children rushed into the burrow shouting "The tomte is here, he's here!" Grandfather did not start singing.

"Stop that," he said. "It is not funny."

And Father did not run to get his hat. He sighed and looked miserable.

"I don't know if I believe in the tomte any longer. Perhaps he doesn't even exist," he said.

"Of course he does," said Mother. "After all the trouble we've gone to. Who else is going to have all these presents?"

"And who else is going to listen to my song?" said Grandfather. "Anyway, that bit of wood we found – it told us he was coming. TOMTE CO, it said."

"Yes, of course," said Father. "But CO might not mean COMING to the forest. It might mean COMING to the city. Or COMING to the Sahara. Or anywhere at all."

He said that, even though he had no idea where the Sahara was. He had only heard the name from migrating birds.

"I don't think so," said Barty. "I think it means that the Yule Tomte is coming SOON!"

"Yes, of course that's what it means," agreed Mother.

But Father did not seem convinced. "We shall have to wait and see," he said.

Then he picked up the parcel containing the flag he had made for the tomte. It had been in place of honour beside the hat on the cupboard. He pushed the parcel into a drawer, and looked sadly at his hat.

"I wish I had never heard of the Yule Tomte," said Father Rabbit.

Binny was also looking at the hat, and at her very sad Father. How awful everything had turned out to be! She had destroyed the hat, Father's most precious thing. And the snow rabbit, her best and only present to the tomte, was gone forever.

She tried a little hop. Sometimes a hop can make people happier.

"Well, you seem to be in a good mood," grumbled Father. "Can't you see how upset I am?"

Binny went into the larder. She wanted to be left alone. She sat among the nut biscuits, the lingonberry loaves, the corn crackers and the barrels of blueberry juice, and felt sorry for herself.

Then Barty came tiptoeing in.

"Are we playing hide and seek?" he asked.

"No," said Binny. "I just want to be alone. It's all my fault!"

"Nothing is your fault," he answered. "Have a carrot cupcake. It will make you feel better. They've made too many, anyway."

So she did. First she took one, and then she took another.

"They're delicious," she said.

"Yes. Happy Christmas!" said Barty.

And they laughed.

20

As the days went by, they all became more irritated.

"If that tomte doesn't come soon, he might as well not come at all," said Binny's sister Abby, and she carried on playing families with a couple of mouse babies. She tucked them into the tomte's grey mittens. Grandfather had said they were sleeping bags, after all.

"Night night, sleep tight," she said.

Father walked about with his hands behind his back, worrying.

"If you think about it, it was all the tomte's fault that my hat got such an ugly stain, because if we had never heard of the Yule Tomte then Binny would never have made a snow rabbit. And if she had never made a snow rabbit it would never have melted. And then there would never have been a stain," he said.

Binny made a decision. She couldn't bear to hear about the hat any more.

She packed a piece of cabbage, a bunch of carrots and a bottle of lingonberry juice. Then she crept to the front door when she thought no one was watching.

But she was wrong. Barty saw her.

"Where are you off to?" he asked.

"Shh! I'm going to get the tomte," she said.

"Then I'm coming with you."

"No," she replied.

"Yes," he said.

"No."

"Yes."

"No."

"Yes."

"All right then," said Binny.

21

The blizzard whipped at their little rabbit faces as they stepped outside.

It rushed through the tree trunks, making the bottle tops rattle on the Christmas tree. Some of the feathers blew away.

It was a terrible storm, but Binny said that was a good thing, because she had heard that the Yule Tomte lived in the place where snow came from.

At least, that was what Owl told them.

"It is good to walk into the wind," Binny said.

It made them feel very tired, but they pretended not to be.

"Oh, how lovely and fresh it is!" yelled Barty.

"Yes, the very best weather for an outing," shouted Binny.

They struggled on. At first they took long hops, then they took shorter ones. And after that they walked. They both agreed that they could see much better when they walked slowly.

"What about going back home?" Barty said, after they had been walking for quite a long time.

Binny turned round to look. Their pawprints had been swept away by the wind, and she did not recognise where they were. They would not be able to find their way home in the storm.

"No," she said. "Not now we're finally out on our big adventure. Hey ho, on we go! I'm sure we'll get to the tomte soon."

When evening came they ate their food.

"Are you tired?" asked Barty.

"No. Not especially."

"Neither am I."

And so they walked on into
the darkness.

22

Grump got up early. He always got up early.

It had snowed all night but now the sky was clear and the stars were shining.

He fetched an armful of corn from the old barn, tied it into a sheaf and fastened it to a stick, which he put outside the kennel window.

Then he sat on his chair with the sleeping bee on his lap, waiting for the birds to appear. He waited for the yellowhammers and the nuthatches, but most of all the bullfinches, because they were such a beautiful red colour. Red, like his hat that blew away.

While he waited, he thought about the dream he had a little while ago, about the woman who said he would have a family. Not one child, but two.

She was about as wrong as she could possibly be, that ghost wrapped up in a nightgown, he thought to himself. And just as well! Where would a tomte get children from?

And, just as he was thinking this, two rabbit children trudged through the gate and up the path.

They were so tired it looked as if they would collapse in a heap at any second.

"We are not taking them in," Grump said irritably to the bumble-bee. "Not for all the porridge in the world."

Then he put the bee in its box and opened the door.

"Go away!" he shouted.

Binny and Barty stopped, turned around and started trudging back towards the gate.

"Goodness gracious, where are you going?" Grump called. "Come here this very minute!"

They turned around again and walked back towards the kennel.

When they stepped inside the door, Binny stared Grump straight in the face.

"Are you the tomte?" she asked.

"That is none of your business," he answered.

"We have come to get you," Barty said.

"I am not going anywhere," Grump said.

But he did. He went to the stove and put on a bowl of water so that Binny and Barty could have a warm bath. They were so cold their teeth were chattering. Then he gave them some warm food and fetched blankets so they could go to sleep.

"Oh deary, deary me, what a nuisance this is," Grump muttered as he trotted off to the house to find the blankets.

"If it isn't bees then it is lost rabbit children. It is one thing after another, and only me to take care of everything."

23

In the burrow in the forest they discovered that Binny and Barty were missing. They had been missing one whole long, black night. And almost a whole day too.

"What were they doing, going out in that bad weather?" wailed Mother Rabbit.

"Binny has always had strange ideas," said Abby.

"I only hope the raven hasn't taken them," said Grandfather.

"Don't talk nonsense," said Auntie Bunty. "I expect they went out to make a den out of branches, and got lost."

Father Rabbit was sitting with his hat resting on his knees. He was crying, and as the tears dripped down they made ugly new stains on the lining.

"Did I go on too much about the hat?" he said. "Perhaps I made Binny sad when I said it was stupid to put a snow rabbit in it."

"Well, you did make her sad," said Mother. "Put that wretched hat away now."

So Father put it in the cupboard.

Then he put his paw on Grandfather's shoulder.

"I miss them so much," he sighed. "Can you work out what to do? You are so very good at thinking."

"I can try," said Grandfather. He thought for a while with one paw pressed to his nose, and then he said:

"If you think about someone a lot then I believe that the rabbit – or whatever creature it is – can feel it. So, if we sit in a circle, and hold each other's paws, and think of Binny and Barty, maybe they'll feel it and find their way home again."

Everyone thought that was a brilliant idea.

They all held paws – the rabbits, the badger, the hedgehog, the squirrel, the mice; in fact, everyone except the mice babies who were asleep in their sleeping bags – and thought of Binny and Barty.

They remembered all the fun they had together, the way they tumbled about in the summer grass, and how little they were when they were little.

From time to time someone peered outside to see if they were coming, but each time the animal came back and shook its head.

"It is starting to get dark already," said Father.

One of the bounciest young rabbits went out to do a few somersaults.

Then he stuck his head in the burrow and called:

"The tomte is coming! He's here now!"

"Stop your messing about," said Father sternly.

24

But it really was the Yule Tomte! With a sock on his head. He had Binny and Barty with him too. And the bee in its little box.

They were on a sledge that Grump found in the woodshed. It was being pulled by the fox and because it was Christmas Eve the fox had promised to be kind and not eat anyone up. Grump had hung a lantern at the front of the sledge, and small brass bells that jingled and jangled. After all, a tomte cannot arrive any old how.

"Happy Christmas! Here I come with your youngsters!" he called.

"Here we come with the tomte!" shouted Binny and Barty.

Binny and Barty climbed down and were hugged by Mother and Father, as the rabbit children and the mice and the voles presented themselves to the tomte all at once.

"Stop it! What is all this noise?" he spluttered, but quite kindly.

"Presentations, presentations! That's what you have at Christmas," they said.

Father Rabbit went and put on his hat so that he would be able to lift it off and bow.

"You are most heartily welcome, dear Tomte," he said. "And thank you for bringing our children."

Grump took off his sock and bowed, too.

"I certainly did not want them staying with me," he replied.

Then Grandfather sang his song. He sang it twice, because it was so short:

"Oh, snow so white and night so clear,
Such fun, Mr Tomte, to have you here.
We can eat till we can eat no more,
Christmas has come now you're at our door!"

There was dancing round the Christmas tree. Then they all went into the burrow and ate pine nut pies and root spaghetti, mushroom and chestnut stew, rosehip biscuits and carrot cupcakes and rowanberry jelly, until they couldn't eat another mouthful.

Then it was time to give the tomte his presents, and the one that made him happiest of all was the red flag: his very own tomte hat.

"Thank you, everyone," he said. "Just what I needed, and exactly the right size. This is my best Christmas for a hundred years."

"Ours too!" said Binny. "But may I ask you something?"

"Yes, if it will not take too long to answer," said Grump.

"Why do we celebrate Christmas?"

"Because a child has come to earth," said the tomte.

"Then we can celebrate twice as much," said Father, "because two children came to us!"

And he looked at Binny and Barty.

"HAPPY CHRISTMAS!" he shouted, and threw his hat in the air. The bee woke up and flew into the air as well.

25

When all the others finally went to bed, giddy from the dancing, happiness and good food, Grump crept out of the burrow with a shovel in his hand. He scraped snow into a big pile and packed it down very, very hard. In the moonlight it looked like half a moon peeping out of the ground.

He fetched buckets of water and poured them over the mound of snow.

When morning came, the mound had turned to ice in the bitter cold. Grump chopped open a doorway and shovelled out all the loose snow, until all that was left was a huge bowl made of ice.

Then he lit candles inside.

When he was finished, he woke everyone up.

"Up you get!" he roared. "Time for the morning service!"

"Morning service? What's that?" asked Binny.

"It is a special occasion," said Grump. "You sit still in a special place. There is no dancing. No eating. No presentations. All you do is sit and be happy. It is perfectly all right to keep quiet. But you may sing, too. Now, hurry up, and bring something to sit on!"

Everyone found cushions of grass and moss, and they made their way to the tomte's ice house.

"Oh!" they said. And "Imagine!" and "Well I never!" – because it was the most beautiful thing they had ever seen.

The stars twinkled through the icy roof, and the candles glowed on the floor. There they sat, feeling happy about all the children that had

ever been born. They had given the Yule Tomte presents, and now he had given them something very special in return.

The birds sang, and the bee hummed. But most of the animals sat in silence. They sat there until the sun came up and painted the whole ice bowl red. Then Grump stood up and tiptoed to the doorway.

"Will you come back again next year?" Binny asked.

"I might," he said in a kind voice.

"Or I might not," he added.

Because at that very moment, he remembered that he was supposed to be grumpy.